ATTACK OF THE
UNDERWEAR DRAGON

written by
SCOTT ROTHMAN

illustrations by
PETE OSWALD

Random House 🏠 New York

Cole had always wished he could be an assistant knight to Sir Percival—his favorite knight of King Arthur's Round Table.

So Cole wrote him a letter:

Dear Sir Percival,
I would make a
great assistant knight
because I am smart,
I work hard, and
whatever I don't
know, I promise to
learn. Please give
me a shot.

Cole

Sir Percival read Cole's letter . . . and cried. That's right. Knights cry.

Knights cry at sad plays
and bad plays . . .

when they step on
something sharp

or run into a harp . . .

when they cut onions

or get bunions . . .

when they get stuck
on castle ceilings

or when a wizard hurts their feelings.

But Sir Percival cried because he had once written a letter to his favorite knight, Sir Lancelot—who had given him a shot.

So Sir Percival made Cole
his assistant knight.

Cole had a lot to learn.
He learned how to sharpen Sir Percival's swords . . . spears . . .
battle-axes . . . and knight pencils.

He learned how to ride a horse . . .

. . . and swing a sword.

How to paint Sir Percival doing awesome knight poses . . .

and calm Sir Percival when he awoke from nightmares about a big, scary Underwear Dragon.

Cole learned how to get knocked off a horse . . .

knocked down by a knight . . .

knocked over by a princess . . .

and knocked out by a catapult.

At battle time, Cole learned how to pack Sir Percival's stuff . . . lug it to battle . . .

cheer for Sir Percival when the battle began . . .

. . . and bandage his boo-boos
when it was all over.

Cole loved learning what made Sir Percival a great knight (even if Sir Percival
was terrified an Underwear Dragon would come and destroy the kingdom).

Unfortunately, an Underwear Dragon came and destroyed the kingdom.

All the knights fought the Underwear Dragon, and all the knights lost.

Pretty soon, there was only one knight left.

Pretty soon, there were no knights left.

So Cole wrote another letter:

Dear Underwear Dragon —
I am only an Assistant
Knight of the Round
Table but I think you
should clean up the
mess you made because
it's not nice to mess
up a kingdom that does
not belong to you. I
can help if you want.

♡ Cole

The Underwear Dragon got Cole's letter . . . and ate it.

That's right. Underwear Dragons can't read.

Underwear Dragons can't read letters . . . jesters' sweaters . . . billboards . . .

signs for Gil's Swords . . .

party invitations . . . poems about crustaceans . . . royal decrees . . . bath oil recipes . . .

moat signs . . . goat kinds . . .

menus . . . words with ten U's . . .

or even maps that medieval hens use.

The Underwear Dragon went to eat Cole next.

When Cole saw the Underwear Dragon, he was scared.
And when the Underwear Dragon attacked, Cole didn't think
he would be able to do anything.

But then, Cole remembered everything he'd learned
from being an assistant knight . . .

and fought . . .

and jousted . . .

and wrestled . . .

and catapulted the Underwear Dragon . . .

. . . until its underwear flew off.

And so did the dragon.

The whole kingdom cheered and helped Cole clean up the mess the Underwear Dragon had made.

Back at his castle, King Arthur made Cole a knight
and gave him a place at the Round Table.

But Sir Cole just wanted
to get some rest . . .

KINGDOM TIMES

HERO
SAVES THE DAY!

GOLDEN
UNDERWEAR
AWARD

because tomorrow he needed
to find his own assistant
knight of the Round Table.

For Ella, Cole, and Maxwell
—S.R.

For Sir Vincent
—P.O.

Text copyright © 2020 by Scott Rothman
Jacket art and interior illustrations copyright © 2020 by Pete Oswald

Visit us on the Web! rhcbooks.com

Educators and librarians, for a variety of teaching tools, visit us at RHTeachersLibrarians.com

Library of Congress Cataloging-in-Publication Data
Names: Rothman, Scott, author. | Oswald, Pete, illustrator.
Title: Attack of the Underwear Dragon / by Scott Rothman ; illustrated by Pete Oswald.
Description: First edition. | New York : Random House Children's Books, [2020] | Audience: Ages 3–7. | Audience: Grades K–1. |
Summary: When a dragon wearing very large underwear threatens the kingdom, the Knights of the Round Table run away,
leaving Sir Percival's young assistant, Cole, to face the beast.
Identifiers: LCCN 2019040341 (print) | LCCN 2019040342 (ebook) | ISBN 978-0-593-11989-1 (hardcover) |
ISBN 978-0-593-11990-7 (library binding) | ISBN 978-0-593-11991-4 (ebook)
Subjects: CYAC: Knights and knighthood—Fiction. | Apprentices—Fiction. | Dragons—Fiction. | Humorous stories.
Classification: LCC PZ7.1.R762 Att 2020 (print) | LCC PZ7.1.R762 (ebook) | DDC [E]—dc23

Book design by Nicole de las Heras

MANUFACTURED IN CHINA
10 9 8 7 6 5 4 3 2 1
First Edition